WITHDRAWN
FROM
STOCK

First published in 1996
by Macdonald Young Books

Text copyright © Stephen Bowkett 1996
Illustrations copyright © Stephen Player 1996

This edition re-issued in 2008 by Wayland

Wayland
338 Euston Road
London NW1 3BH

Wayland Australia
Level 17/207 Kent Street
Sydney, NSW 2000

British Library Cataloguing in Publication Data available

ISBN: 978 0 7502 5417 5

Printed in China

Wayland is a division of Hachette Children's Books,
an Hachette Livre UK company

THE WORLD'S SMALLEST WEREWOLF

STEPHEN BOWKETT

Illustrated by Stephen Player

WAYLAND

Chapter One

It was Tom and Ellie's big adventure. They were really excited to be visiting Louis in the wilds of Scotland. Louis had been their pen-pal for three years and they were great friends by letter, but this was the first time they'd met. Would they like Louis as much in person? Tom and Ellie felt a little nervous as they picked up their bags and stood by the door ...

The train came to a stop in front of a sign which said: *GLENBARRA – Dumfries & Galloway Region*. Even at first glance, it seemed like a small town in the middle of nowhere.

"Look!" said Ellie. "There's Louis now!" She and Tom started waving. Louis, a rather small and anxious-looking boy with straight dark hair, waved back.

Louis' father, Grant Garou, opened the carriage door. Unlike his son, Mr Garou

was a huge man with
strong hairy arms and a
shaggy black beard. He
stared at the Tyler
children with bright,
sharp eyes. And Ellie
noticed anger in them, and perhaps a little
fear too, which she thought was
rather odd.

Tom rather shyly said hello. Ellie smiled
at Louis. "It's lovely to meet you at last,"
she said, her voice shaking slightly.

"Yes," Mr Garou answered in a growly kind of voice. "We'll see …"

Louis glanced at his father uncertainly, and said nothing.

Mr Garou walked ahead with the bags and the children followed. Ellie couldn't help but notice that all of the people stopped to stare at them. Just like we're *strange*, and not just strangers … she thought uneasily.

They came out through the station entrance into beautiful autumn sunlight. Mr Garou's truck was parked close by. Louis had  said in his letters that his father was a forester, and spent days away working in the vast pine timberlands surrounding the town.

Ellie gasped at the wonderful, breathtaking scenery. In the distance, tall mountains reached to the sky. Down in the wide valley, Glenbarra was a cluster of buildings following the river. It was all so sunny, so *open* – and yet the people seemed very dark and shadowy; not happy at all.

Tom pointed out another town that was some miles away in the distance.

"That's Castle Rock," Louis explained. "Perhaps we'll go there to shop! And look —" he indicated a colourful patch close to the river. "The funfair's come to town! Maybe …" Then he stopped, looked anxiously at his father again, and became silent.

They piled into Mr Garou's truck and headed for home. Passing through the town's main street, the children noticed a huge coloured poster nailed to a fence.

JEREMIAH DARK'S FUNFAIR AND TRAVELLING SHOW

Roll up! Roll up! See the amazing Vampire Boy – the astonishing Reptile Woman – the Living Mummy from Ancient Egypt – the Human Spider ... and a new addition – the World's Smallest Werewolf – PLUS your favourite Rides and Games – ROLL UP! ROLL UP! ROLL UP!!

Mr Garou snarled angrily. "Do you see what they're doing, son?" he barked at Louis. "They're making fun of people who are different from themselves. It's disgusting! It should be stopped!"

Tom and Ellie looked shocked at this outburst. Louis just hung his head in dismay.

Chapter Two

"I think we got off to a bad start," Ellie whispered, as she and Tom left their bedroom and started down the stairs.

It was an hour later. They had met Louis' mother – a kindly lady, but as quiet and as secretive as everyone else in Glenbarra. After their meal, they asked if they could explore for themselves. Mr Garou grunted a reply. "But don't wander too far – and make sure you're back by nightfall."

"Can Louis come with us?" Ellie asked hesitantly.

"It's not safe —" Mrs Garou started to say.

Her husband glanced at her quickly. "No, he cannot. Louis has some jobs to do around the house. You go – but remember what I said."

"Well I hope the rest of the visit isn't

going to be like this!" Tom muttered unhappily to his sister.

They reached the bottom of the stairs and were just about to walk to the door, when they heard Louis' voice coming from the kitchen. He sounded terribly upset.

"I did the wrong thing, didn't I? I shouldn't have invited them," he said, with a little sob of sadness.

"No, son. I think you did the right thing, but maybe at the wrong time. We have tried to keep the world out for long enough. Times are changing. But it's hard not to be frightened of people. After all, they'd be frightened of us."

Someone knocked
gently at the back door.
Mrs Garou answered it.
Several men were standing
there. They were all big,
like Louis' dad, and all had shaggy beards
and long hair. They came in silently,
towering over Louis
and filling the room.

Mr Garou spoke
solemnly. "Well, you've all
seen that so-called
'funfair', with its
specimens and freaks –
and now little Harriet
Brandner is missing … So, I guess we all
know what must be done."

One of the men, who had reddish hair
and a wide, angry grin, leaned forward
across the table. "Yes, Grant, we're with
you. Will it be
tonight?"

"Tonight," Grant Garou agreed gruffly.
"Before the fair moves on."

The red-haired man said, "And what about the human children, little Louis' friends?"

They all stared at Louis, who gazed back, wide-eyed and frightened.

"Let's just hope they don't get in the way," Mr Garou told them softly.

Tom and Ellie held their breath as they listened from the stairs. Now, as they let out a shuddering sigh, Ellie looked anxiously at her brother.

"What's going on, Tom? What does he mean, '*human* children'?"

Tom frowned in puzzlement and fear. "I'm not sure."

A shadow loomed in the hall and they both jumped.

Louis came through from the kitchen, instantly realizing his two friends had heard everything.

"I can't explain – not yet," he said. "But please trust me. No one will hurt you if you stay out of the way."

Louis dug into his pocket and pressed something into Tom's hand – a strange silver coin with the face of a wolf stamped upon it.

"What's this?" Tom asked. He had never seen anything like it before.

Louis shook his head. "Never mind what it is. Just keep it with you. If anything *unusual* happens, hold it high in the air. Then you'll be safe."

And before the children could question him further, Louis returned to the kitchen and shut the door behind him.

Chapter Three

Ellie and Tom could see plenty of people going to the fair from Castle Rock. But no one, apart from themselves, was walking along the road out of Glenbarra.

"What's going on?" Ellie muttered, shaking her head at the mystery.

"And who's Harriet Brandner?" Tom wondered as he glanced again at the silver coin Louis had given them. "Do you suppose she's been kidnapped?"

Ellie was about to reply, but then both of them froze as they heard an eerie, soulful sound echoing through the trees nearby.

Ellie's eyes went wide with fright.

As the children listened, the sound came again. Tom and Ellie turned towards the huge dark forest spreading over the hills. And for a third time the weird sound echoed around them.

Ellie's mouth quivered.
"T – Tom … That
howling – it's …"
"I know," Tom
whispered fearfully. *It's the
howling of wolves!"*

They hurried on towards the bright
lights of the funfair. It felt safer being
closer to all the noise and crowds. When
Tom looked back along the road, he saw a
huge full moon rising above Glenbarra. By
its light, watching them from the
roadside, was a great red-furred wolf ...

Chapter Four

When they reached the funfair, they had a turn on the coconut shy and the dodgem cars. Then Ellie insisted they try the helter-skelter. After that, Tom wanted a hot dog. Then they both bought a cola, before riding on the carousel.

At last, bright-faced and giggling, they turned a corner and found themselves in a much quieter part of the fair. There were no crowds here, just rows of caravans and trailers, some empty cages and boxes stacked on top of each other.

Ellie's smile slowly faded. "We came the wrong way, Tom. This is the back of the funfair."

She paused as a mournful squeal drifted

eerily through the air; then pointed
towards a shabby tent nearby. "It's coming
from there."

"That must be where they keep the
human spider and the vampire boy!"
There was excitement in Tom's voice.

Ellie looked at her brother seriously.
"That's what Mr Garou hated so much.
All those poor things locked up for people
to goggle at. It isn't right."

"I'll bet they're all fakes, anyway," Tom replied with a sneer. "I think they'll all just be dummies or dolls."

"Well let's find out," Ellie told him, "and put our minds at rest!"

They walked between two huge trailers to the front of the tent. A bored-looking man sat at the entrance. Ellie paid for herself and Tom, and they went inside.

The lights were dim and the cages and display cases were half in shadow.

"I told you so." Tom pointed to the "Reptile Woman". It was obviously built of papier mâché, poorly painted to look like a monster. The "Vampire Boy" was nothing more than a tailor's dummy with silly plastic fangs stuck on. And the "Human Spider" was made of rope, tied around a painted doll.

Ellie smiled as they walked on. "OK Tom, you were right …"

Then they came to the cage of the "World's Smallest Werewolf". And there, its tiny paws gripped around the bars,

knelt a tiny wolf-child with the saddest eyes the children had ever seen.

Ellie put her hand to her mouth to stifle a cry. "Oh Tom – it's real … It really is a werewolf!"

The little creature cocked its head and opened its mouth. Its teeth were white and sharp and perfect. It whimpered pitifully.

"It's only a baby!" Tom was suddenly furious. His eyes were hot with tears and temper. "The poor thing's been taken from its parents and thrown in this cage and left … It's Jeremiah Dark who's the monster!" Tom shouted. "And I'm going to do something about it!"

"I bet this is Harriet Brandner!" said Ellie suddenly. "Don't you see, Tom – there must be a family of wolf-people living near Glenbarra and the rest of the townsfolk are trying to protect them!"

"But werewolves are wild and fierce and – and – they eat people, Ellie!"

"You've only read about that in books," Ellie said. "How do you know for sure – have you ever met a real werewolf?"

"Only this one." Tom gave a faint, wavering smile. "Though I'm not sure I'd want to meet her father—"

Both children jumped as something loomed up from behind the werebaby's cage. Something huge, red-eyed and fierce—

A werewolf, twice the size of a man, with teeth like knives. Its gigantic hands reached down and pulled the bars aside as though they were made of toffee. It snatched the tiny werewolf up, roared at Tom and Ellie, then disappeared from sight.

Chapter Five

In the next instant there was a commotion outside. Men were shouting and torchlights flickered around the tent.

Tom grabbed Ellie's hand. "Quick, follow me. We don't want to be blamed for this."

The huge werewolf had torn his way through the back of the tent. Tom led Ellie through the rip. They began running down the narrow space between rows of lorries and caravans.

Before they reached the end, a crowd of angry-looking men blocked their way. One of them pointed.

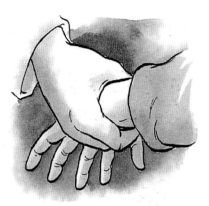

"There, Jeremiah! There are the thieves!"

The men, armed with sticks and firebrands, charged forward.

"This way!" Ellie hissed. She dragged Tom under a parked lorry and out the other side. The way was clear.

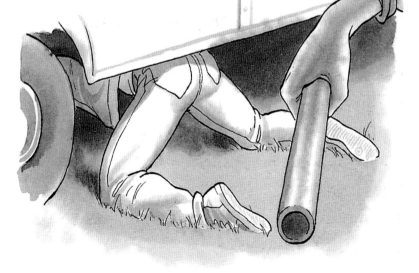

Until suddenly, three massive
werewolves jumped down from the top of
the lorry and surrounded them.

Ellie shrieked, and Tom's heart gave a
great leap of fright. There was no escape.

The wolves closed in, their jaws gaping
wide, their red tongues panting, their eyes
glinting in the moonlight like polished
coins ...

Coins, Tom thought, suddenly remembering. *Polished coins!*

He pulled Louis' silver coin from his pocket and held it high.

"Don't hurt us," he said loudly. "We don't mean you any harm."

One of the beasts growled something. The others nodded their great shaggy heads.

And before Tom and Ellie could do anything further, two werewolves had scooped them up on their backs.

Chapter Six

With the children clinging desperately to their long fur, the powerful creatures ran as fast as a speeding car under the moonlit sky, away from the funfair and the shouting men, through the dark forest, and into Glenbarra.

They went straight to the square at the end of the main street. And there the people of the town were waiting.

And all of them were werewolves.

At the front of the crowd, Grant Garou
stood and watched. His teeth glinted.
Nearby, a female wolf nestled the
werebaby in her arms. It seemed
contented at last.

Only Louis was in his human shape. He
looked worried as Tom and Ellie were
gently lowered to the ground by the
werewolves.

There were a few seconds of silence, then Louis held out his hands. "So now you know our secret …" As he spoke, his body seemed to shiver and change. And he too stood in his wolf-shape, silver and black.

"We are in your power," Grant Garou added. "If people like Jeremiah Dark found out about us, he would try to put us *all* in cages!"

The crowd murmured and growled, a low, nervous sound.

"We have lived here for so long," Louis went on. "Keeping ourselves to ourselves. And we have been so frightened. Mankind has mistrusted us for centuries; hunted us down. We just want to live in peace."

Ellie smiled. "We won't tell on you. Will we, Tom?"

"No," Tom agreed, "we'd never do that. We understand now that not all werewolves are fierce and evil."

"And neither are you!"
Louis chuckled, sounding
like a small shy boy once
more.

Ellie gave him a hug.

Tom strode up to Grant Garou, who
grinned, reached down and gripped Tom's
fingers in his vast, black-clawed paw.

And they shook hands, as equals and
friends.

Look out for more creepy titles in the Tremors series:

The Curse of the Ghost Horse by Anthony Masters

Jake believes the ghost tale of Black Bess, a horse that fell to her death when forced to jump a huge crevasse. He is convinced the ghost horse is cursing his family and is determined to jump the crevasse to find Black Bess. But will Jake's obsession lead to his death...?

The Headmaster's Ghost by Sam Godwin

It's the school trip to Mortimer Hall. Adam and Melissa decide to scare Danny senseless by telling him the story of the evil headmaster's ghost who haunts the house. Danny is determined to show he isn't scared. But does his determination bring him more than he bargained for...?

Terror in the Attic by Barbara Mitchelhill

A lodger has rented the attic in Craig and Kelly's house, but there is something odd about him. Why does he always dress in black? What is in his leather bag? Desperate to solve the mystery of this stranger they decide to explore the attic. But does their curiosity get the better of them...?

Danny and the Sea of Darkness by David Clayton

One minute Danny's lying in bed, the next he's thrashing about in a foaming sea. Why does he keep going back as Michael? And what will happen when he returns to the Sea of Darkness once more?

All these books and many more in the Tremors series can be purchased from your local bookseller. For more information about Tremors, write to: *The Sales Department, Hachette Children's Books, 338 Euston Road, London NW1 3BH*